Which Animals

Suck Their Thumbs?

Written by Kimberly Selzman
Illustrated by Katherine Lloyd

ISBN: 1-4392-0709-7
ISBN-13: 9781439207093

Visit www.booksurge.com to order additional copies.

Dedicated to Zachary (and his right thumb) for the inspiration and to his Dad for unwavering support and patience —KAS

Do any animals suck their thumb like me?

I wonder if giraffes suck their thumbs or put their fingers in their mouth?

No!
Giraffes don't have fingers or thumbs. They have hooves that they use for walking around.

Does a tiger put her fingers in her mouth?

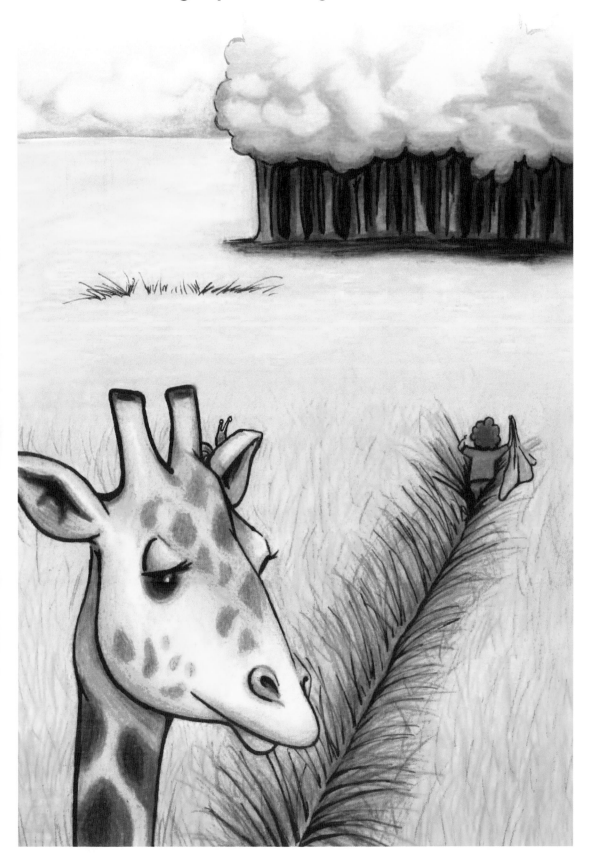

No!
A tiger has paws that she uses for climbing in the trees.

Well... does a seal like to put his fingers in his mouth?

No!
A seal has flippers that he uses for swimming.

I know...maybe an octopus puts all his thumbs in his mouth!

No! An octopus does not have any thumbs. An octopus has eight arms for slithering along slippery rocks on the sea floor.

I wonder if eagles suck their thumbs?

No!
Eagles don't have thumbs! They have wings that they use for flying high in the sky.

Let me see... Do bears put their claws in their mouths?

No!
A bear uses her claws to eat honey or blueberries.

Maybe a spider likes to put its fingers in its mouth?

No! A spider does not have fingers. A spider has eight long legs to crawl around with.

Hmmm... Does a dolphin put her fins in her mouth?

No!
A dolphin uses her fins to dive in and out of the water.

Well... do crabs put their hands in their mouths?

NO silly! Crabs have claws that they use to grab things.

I need to check if any elephants suck their thumb!

Nope. Elephants do not have any thumbs either. Elephants have long trunks that they use to pick up their food and put it in their mouth.

So I guess animals use their

hooves,
claws
and paws

to run,
eat
and crawl!

What are your fingers and thumbs for?

They are for...

Climbing

Drawing

Eating

Pointing

Catching and Throwing

And for petting your favorite animal!

Kimberly Selzman is a practicing physician and she is also a recovered childhood thumbsucker. This is her first children's book. She lives in Utah with her husband and two children, Zachary and Sofia.

Katherine Lloyd is a Studio Art and English Major from the University of North Carolina at Chapel Hill. This is her first children's book illustration, but picture books greatly inspired her as a child and she hopes to make many more.

7177013R0